The Secret Garden

Retold by
Annabel Savery

Illustrated by
Mel Howells

ARCTURUS

For my A-Team—AS.

For The Crouch Enders—MH.

ARCTURUS

This edition published in 2018 by Arcturus Publishing Limited
26/27 Bickels Yard, 151–153 Bermondsey Street,
London SE1 3HA

Writer: Annabel Savery
Illustrator: Mel Howells
Designer: Jeni Child
Editor: Becca Clunes
Art Director: Jessica Crass

ISBN: 978-1-78828-693-0
CH006180NT
Supplier 24, Date 0318, Print run 6740

Printed in Malaysia

Contents

CHAPTER 1

"That's th' moor"

When Mary Lennox was sent to to live with her uncle, everybody said she was a most disagreeable-looking child. She had a pale face, a little thin body, and a sour expression. Mary had been born in India to parents who were too taken up with work and parties to be bothered with a troublesome child. She was left in the care of a nurse, her Ayah, who gave the child her every wish. By the time Mary was six years old, she was as tyrannical and selfish a little girl as ever lived.

When she was nine years old, the cholera struck the small army compound they lived on. The few who survived soon fled, and Mary found herself quite alone in the world. She was sent to Misselthwaite Manor in England to live with her mother's brother, Mr. Archibald Craven.

Through boats, trains, and carriages, Mary listened to people talking and heard that her uncle was a misery-ridden hunchback, and the house was great and gloomy. Eventually, she arrived and met the housekeeper, Mrs. Medlock.

"You needn't expect people to talk to you. You'll have to play by yourself, and you're not to go poking about."

"I shall not want to go poking about," said sour little Mary.

She was led up a broad staircase, down a long corridor, and around a great many corners, until she found herself in a room with a fire and a supper on a table.

"This is your room, and make sure you keep to it," Mrs. Medlock said.

*

When Mary woke up the next morning, she saw Martha, a young housemaid, lighting the fire. Out of the window, Mary could see a great stretch of bare land.

"That's th' moor," Martha said smiling. "I just love it. It's covered wi' growin' things as smells sweet."

She was a strange servant, but Mary was amused at the way she rattled on about her family of twelve living in a small cottage with

little to eat and her brother Dickon, who
was a great lover of animals. Martha was just
as bemused by the little girl from India, who
held her arms out expecting to be dressed
and refused her good hot porridge.

"Wrap up warm, an' run out an' play,
it'll do you good," said Martha, handing
her a coat and stout pair of boots. "Mind,"
she whispered, "one of th' gardens is
locked up. Ten year ago, Mr. Craven
locked th' door an' buried th' key."

The gardens looked dull and lifeless in the winter sunlight. Mary was curious about the garden that no one had been into for ten years. She wondered whether there were any flowers still alive in it. She turned down a grass walk that led to a door in an old wall, and soon, she came upon an old man digging.

"What is your name?" Mary inquired.

"Ben Weatherstaff," he grumbled, continuing to dig.

"What is this place?" she asked.

"One o' th' kitchen gardens," he answered shortly.

"There's another on t'other side o' th' wall, an' th' orchard t'other side o' that."

She heard a soft little rushing noise, and a bird with a red breast alighted on the earth near the gardener's foot. He had soft, bright eyes, a tiny plump body, and slender, delicate legs.

"What's that bird?" she whispered.

"He's a robin redbreast. They're th' friendliest, curiousest birds alive. He's always comin' to see what I'm plantin'."

The robin hopped about, busily pecking the soil. His little black eyes gazed at Mary with great curiosity. Then, the next moment, the robin flew away.

Mary went down the path and through the second green door. She found winter vegetables and bare fruit trees. The wall went on past the orchard, and she could see the tops of trees above it. The wall here was covered with ivy growing all over it. Above her head, there was a burst of song, and she looked up to see the robin.

"I believe that bird is in the secret garden," she said. "There is a wall around the place, but there is no door."

CHAPTER 2

"There was someone crying!"

From that first day, the many days that came and went seemed exactly alike to Mary. Every morning, she was woken by Martha, she ate a small breakfast and went out. As she ran along the paths, she was making herself stronger and healthier. The air of the moor filled her lungs, her eyes began to grow bright, and her cheeks began to grow pink.

Each day, she explored the garden, but most days, she came back to the one part of the wall where the ivy was not so neatly trimmed. She saw the robin there, and he chirruped to her. But explore as she might, she couldn't get into the garden where he was.

One day, the rain poured down in torrents, and Mary could not go outside. She thought that there must be a hundred rooms in the great house, and she made up her mind to explore. She slipped out of her room and wandered down the corridors, looking at portraits of little girls in long frocks and little boys in lace collars. Suddenly, the stillness was broken by a strange sound.

"It is crying," thought Mary, her heart beating faster. "And it is quite close."

The next moment, Mrs. Medlock appeared from behind a tapestry that must have concealed a door.

"What are you doing here?" she said, pulling Mary away by the arm.

"I was lost, and I heard someone crying." Mary explained.

"You didn't hear anything of the sort," said the housekeeper. She took Mary by the arm, until she had pushed her through the door of her own room.

"You stay where you're told to, or you'll find yourself locked up!" She slammed the door, leaving Mary pale with rage.

"There was someone crying!" she said to herself.

Two days after this, the rainstorm ended, the wind ceased, and a brilliant, deep-blue sky arched high over the moorland. Never had Mary dreamed of a sky so blue.

"Look at the moor!" she called to Martha when she woke.

"Aye," said Martha cheerfully. "Th' storm's over, an' th' springtime's on its way." Martha stared at her a

moment—the small plain face did not look quite so sour this morning.

Mary went out into the garden. She found Ben Weatherstaff working in the kitchen garden.

"Springtime's comin,'" he said. "You'll see bits o' green spikes stickin' out o' th' black earth after a little. You watch."

"I am going to," answered Mary. She wanted to know very much if things might be stirring in the locked-up garden, but she didn't dare ask the grumpy gardener.

Mary went to the long, ivy-covered wall over which she could see the treetops. She heard a chirp and a twitter, and when she looked at the bare flower bed, there was the robin.

"Do you remember me?" she whispered. "You do!"

The robin hopped over a small pile of earth freshly turned up by a dog looking for a mole. It was quite a deep hole, and as Mary looked at it, she saw something almost buried in the newly turned soil. It was a rusty metal ring. She picked it up to find that it was an old key, which looked as if it had been buried for a long time.

"Perhaps it has been buried for ten years," she said in a whisper. "Perhaps it is the key to the garden!"

If it was the key to the locked garden, and she could find out where the door was, she could perhaps open it and see what had happened to the old rose trees. She made up her mind that she would always carry it with her, so that if she ever should find the hidden door, she would be ready.

CHAPTER 3

"How still it is!"

Later that week, Martha went home to visit her mother, and Mary was surprised

that she missed the lively housemaid. When Martha returned, she had brought a present for Mary.

"It's a skipping rope," she said.

"Look, I'll show you how to use it!"

Mary took the rope out into the garden. She was not very clever at jumping at first, but she liked it so much that she skipped until her cheeks were quite red. As had become her habit, she went to her own special walk, and there was the robin, swaying on a long branch of ivy.

"You showed me where the key was," she said. "You ought to show me the door today!"

Mary had heard a great deal about Magic in Indian stories, and later, she always said that what happened at that moment was Magic. As the robin flew up to the top of the wall, a little gust of wind rushed down the walk. The trailing ivy swayed, and Mary jumped and caught some in her hand. She had seen something underneath it.

Mary pulled the leaves aside, her heart thumping and her hands shaking in her excitement. There was a door. She drew out the key, fitted it in the keyhole. She turned it and looked behind her—no one was coming. She held back the ivy, pushed back the door, and slipped through. She was standing inside the secret garden.

"How still it is!" Mary whispered. "I am the first person here for ten years."

She stood looking around her with excitement and delight. The climbing roses had run all over the walls and trees, but there were neither leaves nor flowers on them now.

"I hope they aren't all completely dead," thought Mary.

She began to walk around the garden. Suddenly, she saw something sticking out of the earth—some little green points.

"Here are tiny growing things," she cried out softly, kneeling down to look at them closely. "Even if the roses are dead, there are other things alive."

She went all around the garden and found there were ever so many more of the sharp, pale green points.

Mary looked at the new shoots. The grass seemed so thick that they did not seem to have room enough to grow. She knelt down and dug, until the shoots had little clear places around them.

"Now they can breathe," she said. "I am going to do ever so many more!"

*

The sun shone down for nearly a week on the secret garden. The bulbs were glad to have space to grow. The sun could warm them, and the rain could reach them, so they began to come alive. Mary dug and pulled up weeds, becoming more pleased with her work every hour.

Then one morning, Mary awoke and knew what it was to be hungry. She took up her spoon and began to eat the hot porridge Martha set before her.

"Why did Mr. Craven hate the garden?" Mary asked curiously.

"It's not to be talked about," Martha began. "It was Mrs. Craven's garden, an' she loved it. Him an' her used to stay there for hours, readin' and talkin'. But one day, she was sittin' on an old branch bent like a seat when it broke an' she fell on th' ground. She was hurt so bad that next day she died. No one's never gone in since."

CHAPTER 4

"Might I have a bit of earth?"

One day, as Mary sat working in the secret garden, she heard a peculiar whistling sound. She followed the sound out of the garden and to a little woodland. A boy was sitting under a tree playing a rough wooden pipe. His cheeks were as red as poppies, and his eyes were as blue as the sky. A brown squirrel and two rabbits sat watching him. When he saw Mary, he slowly rose to his feet, and the creatures scampered away.

"I'm Dickon," the boy said. "I know tha'rt Miss Mary." He stooped to pick up a package. "Martha's told me how tha' loves to be in t'garden, so I've brought thee some garden tools."

Mary was so delighted she could hardly speak. They sat down, and he showed her the fork and spade and some packets of flower seeds. He told her what the flowers would look like and how to plant and tend them.

"Has't tha got a bit o' garden?" he asked. Mary said nothing for a time, and then she spoke in a great rush:

"I've stolen a garden. Nobody wants it, nobody cares for it, nobody ever goes into it. Perhaps everything is dead in it already." She said it with such emotion that tears started to form in her eyes.

"Where is it?" asked Dickon. Mary got up at once and pushed aside the ivy that concealed the door.

"Eh! Martha told me there was a locked-up garden," he whispered. He saw her distress at the dead look that everything had. He quickly took out his knife and showed her the live green wood underneath. There would be roses aplenty in the spring, he explained, and all the birds from the moor would love the quiet garden. Then, he spotted one of Mary's own little clearings around the pale green points.

"Who did that there?"

"I did it," said Mary. "The grass was so thick, and they looked as if they had no room to breathe."

"Tha' was right," he smiled. "They'll grow now like Jack's beanstalk. They're crocuses an' snowdrops, an' here's daffy-down-dillys."

"Will you help me again here?" Mary begged. "Oh, do come, Dickon!"

"Aye, I'll come every day," he answered. "It's the best fun I ever had in my life."

"Whatever happens, you never would tell?" Mary said seriously.

"If tha' was a missel thrush an' showed me where thy nest was, does tha' think I'd tell anyone? Not me," he said. And she was quite sure that her secret was safe.

After that, the clock chimed in the courtyard, and Mary had to run in for her midday meal. But she found Mrs. Medlock waiting at the door.

"Mr. Craven wants to see you," she announced. All the pink left Mary's cheeks. She felt herself become her stiff, silent self again. Mrs. Medlock led her to a door and knocked.

"Come in!" sounded a voice, and Mary was ushered inside.

In a chair by the fire sat a man. He had high, rather crooked shoulders and black hair streaked with white. His eyes sank into his face, and his face was lined with sadness.

"Are you well?" he asked. "Do they take good care of you?"

"Yes," answered Mary.

"What do you do all day?" he asked.

Mary's voice trembled. "I play outdoors. I look around for things growing. I don't do any harm."

"Don't look so frightened," he said in a worried voice. "You could not do any harm, a child like you! I cannot give you time or attention; but I wish you to be

happy and comfortable. Is there anything you want?"

"Might I have a little earth?" quavered Mary, and Mr. Craven looked quite startled.

"Earth?!" he repeated.

"To plant seeds in—to make things grow—to see them come alive," Mary faltered. He gazed at her a moment, and his eyes looked far away.

"You remind me of someone else who loved things that grow," he said. "You take a little earth, child, and make it come alive."

"May I take it from anywhere?"

"Anywhere," he answered. "You must go now. I shall be away all summer."

"I can have my garden!" Mary thought with delight. "He is really a nice man, only his face is so miserable."

CHAPTER 5

"Are you a ghost?"

Mary was awakened in the night by the sound of rain beating against her window and wind rushing about the house. Suddenly, something made her sit up in bed and listen, turning her head toward the door.

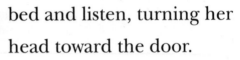

"It isn't the wind, it is crying!" she said in a loud whisper. "I am going to find out what it is."

She picked up her candle and went softly out of the room.

The corridor was long and dark, but faint, far-off crying led her on. At last, she came to the tapestry that concealed a door. She pushed it open.

Mary stared in the darkness. A little candle glowed by the side of a large bed, and on the bed lay a boy, crying. He turned and stared at her. He had a pale white face and wide, pale eyes.

"Are you a ghost?" he said in a frightened whisper.

"No," Mary whispered. "Are you one?"

"No," he replied. "I am Colin. Who are you?"

"I am Mary Lennox. Mr. Craven is my uncle."

"Then, we are cousins! He is my father," said the boy.

"Cousins! Your father!" gasped Mary. "No one told me he had a son!"

"Come closer," he said. "I want to see if you are real."

"I am real. I heard crying and wanted to find out who it was."

"I cry when I can't sleep. Will you come and see me tomorrow? The nurse or Medlock will come any minute. I want to hear more about you, but you shall be a secret—just like they have kept!"

Mary nodded and quickly left the room.

In the morning, Martha appeared, to summon Mary to Colin's room. She was pale and shaking, shocked that he had been discovered. She whispered that he had been ill since he was a baby. He had terrible fits of temper and hysterics, so that the servants were almost terrified of him. His father could not bear to look at him, since his mother had died when he was a baby.

There was a warm fire blazing in Colin's room, and he sat wrapped in a velvet dressing-gown.

"Come in," he commanded. "I want to hear about you."

Colin behaved like a young Indian Rajah, Mary thought, but she sat on a footstool by the bed and told her new cousin about India, the cholera, and her journey to England.

Colin told her about always being ill and how no one believed he would live to grow up. As he spoke, he became more upset and cross.

"Shall I tell you what I've found in the garden?" Mary said, to change the subject.

She talked about green points coming through the earth, about the robin and Ben Weatherstaff, and about Dickon. Colin enjoyed hearing it all, and they talked more than either of them had before. They began to laugh as if they had

been two ordinary creatures—instead of a hard, unloving girl and a sickly boy. And in the midst of the fun, the door opened and in walked Dr. Craven and Mrs. Medlock!

"What is this?" said Dr. Craven, astonished.

"This is my cousin, Mary Lennox," Colin said boldly. "She found me, and I like her. She makes me forget about being ill. She must come and talk to me whenever I send for her."

Mrs. Medlock looked furiously at Mary. Dr. Craven gave a puzzled glance at the stiff, sour little girl. However, neither he nor Mrs. Medlock would oppose the young master, and so, Mary remained.

This first meeting was followed by a whole week of rain, and Mary spent every day with Colin in his room, talking about India or gardens or Dickon or the moor. Mary was careful not to mention the secret garden. She wanted to discover whether Colin was the kind of boy who could keep a secret. She thought he might be, and she had the idea that as gardens and fresh air had been good for her, perhaps they would be good for Colin, too.

Finally, the sky became blue again. Mary woke early and found the spring sunshine irresistible. She ran out to the garden and found Dickon already at work, with a tame fox cub and rook beside him.

The two spent the day working in the secret garden. Mary told Dickon about her meeting with Colin, and they agreed that the warm, spring air was sure to do him good.

The sun was beginning to set when they parted. Mary ran joyfully back to the house to see Colin, but the young Rajah was furious at having been left alone. They raged at each other, each shouting that the other was selfish as could be. Mary went back to her room feeling cross and disappointed.

It was the middle of the night when Mary was awakened by such terrible sounds.

"It's Colin," she said. "He's having one of those dreadful tantrums. How awful it sounds." She put her hands over her ears and felt sick and shivering. "He ought to be stopped!"

Mary jumped out of bed and flew along the corridor.

"You stop!" she shouted. Colin had been lying on his face beating his pillow with his hands.

"I felt the lump—I felt it," he choked. "I shall have a hunch on my back, and then I shall die!"

"You didn't feel a lump!" contradicted Mary fiercely. "There's nothing the matter with your horrid back! Turn over, and let me look at it!"

What she saw was a poor, thin back, and every joint of the spine could be counted.

"There's not a single lump there!" Mary said at last. "There's not a lump as big as a pin—except backbone lumps, and I've got backbone lumps myself!"

No one but Colin himself knew what effect those crossly spoken words had on him. He had never spoken about his secret terrors. He had lain and thought of illness for hours and days and months and years.

"Do you ... think ... think ... I could live ... to grow up?" Colin breathed out.

"Of course!" said Mary, indignantly. "But you must stop your hysterics and have a great deal of fresh air." Colin's tantrum had passed, but he was weak and worn out with crying.

"I'll—I'll go out with you, Mary," he said. "I shan't hate fresh air if you are there."

She turned to go, but Colin pulled her hand. "You could tell me about the gardens and spring—I am sure it will make me go to sleep."

"Of course," answered Mary. "Shut your eyes." He closed his eyes and lay quite still. She talked softly until he fell asleep.

CHAPTER 6

"I want to see it!"

The next morning, Mary went out early, then rushed to Colin's room.

"It has come, the spring!" she said, a little breathless. "Dickon says so!"

"Has it?" cried Colin. "Open the window!" Mary threw it open, and Colin drew in great breaths of fresh air.

"Colin," she said seriously, "can you keep a secret? A truly great secret?" Colin nodded, and Mary went on. "Ten years ago, a garden was locked up. No one was allowed into it, and it has been forgotten. But, I found it!"

"Oh! I want to see it!" he cried out with a half sob. She told Colin how the robin had helped her to find the key and then the door—and how she and Dickon had been working to bring the garden to life. The most important thing, they decided, was that the garden must be kept a secret.

Later that day, the head gardener, Mr. Roach, received orders to remove all his staff from the gardens. The strongest footman carried Colin downstairs and put him in his wheeled chair. He was then dismissed, and Dickon began to push Colin along. The wind swept in soft, big breaths down from the moor, and Colin kept lifting his thin chest to draw it in.

"This is it," breathed Mary as they reached the ivy-covered wall. "Here is the door. Dickon, push him in quickly!"

Colin gasped with delight. Dickon pushed the chair slowly around the garden, stopping every moment to let him look at the wonders springing out of the earth.

All over the walls, a green veil of tender leaves had crept. Here and there were splashes of gold and purple and white. The sun shone softly—warming Colin's ivory face and neck and hands.

"I shall get well! I shall get well!" he cried out.

Mary was a great believer in Magic. Secretly, she believed that Dickon worked Magic and that was why wild creatures liked him so much. She felt that Magic was working and making Colin look like an entirely different boy.

"I don't want this afternoon to end, and I'm going to get fresh air every day," he announced. "I shall get well."

"That tha' will," said Dickon. "Tha's got legs, same as other folks. Us'll have thee walkin' an' diggin' afore long."

They had been quiet for a little while, when Colin half-lifted his head and pointed to the high wall.

"Who is that man?" he whispered. Dickon and Mary scrambled to their feet. Ben Weatherstaff's indignant face was

glaring at them over the wall! He shook his fist at Mary but stopped the very next moment as he saw Colin.

"Do you know who I am?" demanded Colin imperiously.

"Aye, that I do—wi' tha' mother's eyes starin' at me. But tha'rt th' poor cripple, with a crooked back," he said. Colin flushed scarlet, and he sat bolt upright.

"I'm not a cripple!" he cried out furiously. There was a fierce scramble, the rugs were tossed on the ground, Dickon held Colin's arm, the thin legs were out, the thin feet were on the grass.

Poor Ben Weatherstaff choked, and tears ran down his weather-wrinkled cheeks. Dickon held Colin's arm strongly, but the boy stood straighter and straighter.

"I am your master when my father is

away," he said. "This is my garden. Don't dare to say a word about it! Come around to the door, be quick!"

Ben Weatherstaff's crabbed old face obediently disappeared, and when his head was out of sight, Colin turned to Mary and Dickon.

"I can stand!" And as he said it he looked as strong and straight as any other boy.

＊

When Ben Weatherstaff came through the door in the wall, Colin was still standing.

"Look at me!" he commanded Ben Weatherstaff. "Am I a hunchback? Have I got crooked legs?"

"Not tha'," said Ben. "What did tha' shut thysel' up for?"

"Everyone thought I was going to die," said Colin shortly.

"Tha' die!" he said. "Nowt o' th' sort! Tha's got too much pluck in thee. Sit thee down on th' rug a bit, young Mester, an' give me thy orders."

Colin allowed Mary and Dickon to help him sit on a rug under the tree.

"What work do you do in the gardens, Weatherstaff?" he inquired. Ben, they found, had been a gardener to Mrs. Craven. Ben had done his best to tend the locked garden as the years passed, and he would keep their secret.

"How'd tha' like to plant a bit o' somethin'?" said Ben, at last.

"Oh, yes," said Colin, grasping a trowel and turning over some fresh earth. Ben Weatherstaff hobbled out and soon returned, handing a rose in a pot to Colin.

"Here, lad," Ben said. "Set it in the

earth thysel', same as th' king does when he goes to a new place."

The thin white hands shook a little as Colin set the rose in the hole and held it while old Ben made the earth firm.

"It's planted!" said Colin at last. "Help me up, Dickon. The sun is just setting, and I want to be standing when it does. That's part of the Magic."

CHAPTER 7
"I am well"

Dr. Craven continued his visits, but at each, he was dismissed by Colin, who wanted to hear no more of illness and warnings. Each day, the children went into the garden. The seeds Dickon and Mary had planted grew: first showing buds, then opening up into sweet-smelling flowers. The roses climbed up the walls and burst into bloom. Colin watched each change as it took place.

"I am sure there is Magic in

everything," Colin explained one morning. "When Mary found this garden, it looked quite dead. Then, something began pushing things up out of the soil. The Magic in this  garden has made me stand up and know that I am going to live to be a man. I am going to make a scientific experiment."

Dickon and Mary were delighted with the idea, and the three sat in a circle beneath the canopy of the plum tree. Dickon's rabbit, crow, fox, squirrels, and the lamb slowly drew near. It all seemed majestic and mysterious as Colin began:

"The sun is shining—that is the Magic.
The flowers are growing—that is the Magic.
Being alive is the Magic—being strong
is the Magic.
The Magic is in me—the Magic is in me.
Magic! Come and help!"

He said it a great many times, and Mary
listened entranced.

"Now, I am going to walk around the
garden," he announced at last, and so,
a procession was formed. Colin was in
the middle, with Dickon on one side and
Mary on the other.

"The Magic is in me!" Colin kept
saying. "The Magic is making me strong!"

Once or twice, he sat down on the
grass, and several times he paused in the
path and leaned on Dickon, but he would

not give up until he had gone all around the garden.

"I did it! The Magic worked!" he cried. "This is to be the biggest secret of all. No one is to know I have grown so strong, until I can walk and run like any other boy. I won't let my father hear about it. Then, I shall just walk into his study and say: 'Here I am; I am quite well, and I shall live to be a man.'"

"Your father will think he is in a dream," cried Mary.

Every beautiful morning, the Magic was worked by the mystic circle under the plum tree. After the ceremony, Colin did his walking exercise. At first, he needed to sit and rest a lot, but he was determined. After a while, he began to move around as the others did, walking and running and digging and weeding. And each day, his belief in the Magic grew stronger.

With their gain in strength and spirit, Mary and Colin had both begun to worry that their secret would be discovered. They soon made a plan to keep up an appearance of illness and crossness, and to send away all the food that they could bear to. This was a great struggle, until Dickon had a wonderful thought.

Each morning, he brought a tin pail of rich new milk to the garden with him, along with a napkin of fresh rolls from his mother. Poor Dr. Craven and Mrs. Medlock were mystified. The children ate next to nothing, and yet, their faces were rosy and full of life.

"You see, the scientific experiment has succeeded," Colin announced to Ben on his next visit, and all at once, he realized something completely.

"I'm well!" he cried out.

CHAPTER 8

"In the garden"

While the secret garden was coming alive, and two children were coming alive with it, Archibald Craven wandered the beautiful places of Europe. He was filled with sorrow, believing nothing could free him from it.

At the very moment that Colin called out, "I'm well," his father's eyes began to see things he had not seen for years—the tiniest of flowers. Gradually, their beauty filled his mind and softly pushed the darkness aside.

"What is it?" he whispered. "I almost feel as if—I were alive!"

From that moment, his body and his soul began to grow stronger. One night, while in a deep sleep, a voice sounded in his ears. "Archie! Archie!"

"Lilias!" he answered. "Where are you?"

"In the garden," the voice came back, sweet and clear.

"In the garden!" he said, when he awoke. "I must go home at once!"

In a few days, he was in Yorkshire again. On his long journey, he found himself thinking of the past. He remembered the black days when he had raged because the child was alive and the mother was dead. He had not meant to be a bad father. He had supplied doctors and nurses for Colin, but he could not bear to look at his son.

"Ten years is a long time," he thought. "It may be too late to do anything. I will try to find the key," he said. "I will try to open the door. I must—though I don't know why."

He did not go into the house but went straight to the garden. The ivy hung thick over the door that no human being had passed through for ten lonely years—and yet, inside the garden there were sounds: running, scuffling feet and smothered joyous cries.

And then, the feet ran faster and faster, the ivy swung back, the door was flung wide open, and a boy burst through it. Without seeing the outsider, he dashed straight into his arms.

He was a tall boy, and he was glowing with life. He threw the thick hair back

from his forehead and lifted a pair of
strange pale eyes—full of boyish laughter
and rimmed with black lashes. It was the
eyes that made Mr. Craven gasp.

"Who—what? Who!" he stammered.

This was not what Colin planned. But
to come dashing out—perhaps it was
even better. He drew himself up to his
very tallest.

"Father," he said, "I'm Colin. I'm well."

Mr. Craven held the boy's
shoulders and stared
into his face. His
very soul shook with
unbelieving joy.

"In the garden!
In the garden!"
was all that he
could whisper.

"Yes," said Colin. "It was the garden!"

They led Mr. Craven into their garden,
blooming with bright flowers. Mr. Craven
remembered when they had been planted.

"I thought it would be dead," he said.

"Mary thought so at first," said Colin.
"But it came alive."

Then, they sat down under their tree—
all but Colin, who wanted to stand while
he told the story.

It was the strangest thing Archibald Craven had ever heard; mystery and Magic and wild creatures, the midnight meeting, the coming of the spring—and the great secret so carefully kept.

"Now," Colin finished, "it need not be a secret any longer. I am never going to get into the chair again. I shall walk back with you, Father— to the house."

*

Mrs. Medlock had seen the master's carriage arrive, but not the master.

"Did you see Mr. Craven, Weatherstaff?" she asked, when Ben came into the kitchen.

"Aye," he answered slowly. "There's been things goin' on outside as you house people knows nowt about." And it was not two minutes before he waved solemnly toward the window.

"Look there," he said.

Across the lawn came the Master of Misselthwaite. And by his side was a young boy, head up in the air and his eyes full of laughter, walking as strongly and steadily as any boy in Yorkshire—Master Colin.